IN SEARCH OF OUR DREAMS

IN SEARCH OF OUR DREAMS

ROWENA KONG

Contents

I

Retreat

"Thank you so much for each one of your presence here at our offi-cial pre-screening of 'A Maiden's Journey'. I truly hope you have thor-oughly enjoyed this latest feature-length animation, the product of a heartwarming collaboration by all our participating corporations. The story of every dream that has been birthed in our hearts, is worth chas-ing for...No matter how long you have been waiting for, if you keep working out your goals each and every step of the way, dreams will come to pass....Look all around you, and within...the magic might have already begun, and is happening...right here, right now!"

All the audience stood on their feet and applaused as Genny con-cluded the event within the walls of the newly opened grand ballroom of Endearland Gardens. The event purposefully marked its official opening.

When the attendees have proceeded to the luncheon reception, Genny beamed with satisfaction at the success of the pre-screening and snuck away at her chance to join her teammates.

They had earlier talked the guys into taking charge of the rest of the event, while the ladies would go for their deserved afternoon tea retreat back in Gerry's residence.

Once together eagerly and relaxingly chatting away, Trinna had arranged for them all to savour fresh red rose tea delivered on same-day express from Saint Albert's and personally recommended by Genny's grand-aunt, Lady Maybel...

"Oh wonderful, I finally get to breathe once more after months and months of preparation!" Genny declared as she was about to take a light sip of the aromatic beverage.

Everyone smiled empathetically and also relieved that they had done their utmost in helping her.

"Genny, I still wonder if changing the original title of 'A Princess's Journey' really did capture fully the storyline of the show, even though we are not technically 'royalty' to begin with...The word 'Princess' bears connotation for children's animation shows," added Trinna.

Genny understood, "Yes, Trinna. I do agree with you, but you know me, I just get extremely uncomfortable with elevated stature...Really can't help it!"

Aerine nodded and remarked, "It's not only you...we're featured in the show as well! I don't want to be labeled as a spoilt brat!"

Reanne assured them, "Not to worry, they have been kind enough to fulfill our modest request..."

Genny sighed, "You know what, we have indeed come a long way from ten years ago...Now, I can foresee our Endearland Gardens keep boosting visitors until who-knows-when..."

Trinna was ever optimistic, "Finally, I can settle on the choice venue for my long-postponed concert performance!"

All of them heard the first confirmation from her at long last. Genny cried out loud, "Trinna! Why didn't you ever share this secret with me in the first place? Do you know how agonising this must have been for not only me, but every single one of us?"

Trinna carefully set down her fine hand-painted wedgwood teacup and cringed. "So sorry," she could only offer a faint whisper of apology as everyone else got up from their seats to gather around her with folded arms and offended glare.

Aerine gave in, "Trinna, I can't help you this time...We'd really suffered much under Chris's repeated pleadings and demands to know your final decision all these years..."

Trinna sought Reanne's mercy but she only shrugged and shook her head with resignation. "Sis Trinna, even for me, it's too burdensome to bear with him...and you..."

'Arghh..." Trinna bemoaned.

"Ladies, attack!" Genny announced and they all started tickling Trinna on all her sides relentlessly.

2

Planning

"Yes, everything's set and fully arranged for all the children to spend the whole week at Endearland Gardens Village. Their rooms as well as the orphanage staff's - all one hundred of them - will be located on the top five floors of the mansion inn. The children responded to me that their first choice is this major attraction of the whole estate," Genny was speaking to the head overseer of the orphanage over the phone in her study room.

The lady on the line laughed heartily, "You're always taking care of everything so well, just like how Madam Young used to be when she was still around. You've got the genes and inheritance, Genny dear...Our orphanages and the children have never been the same with you around...Wonderful and admirable..."

Genny smiled at her encouraging words, "Thank you, Sister Celestine...But I will still suggest for the children to stay longer for another week or two...The cherry blossoms will be in season by then...The children would definitely get to enjoy the beauty a lot more!"

She was touched by Genny's thoughtfulness and planning, "That's a great idea...We've been extremely busy these days till no one remembers the flowers anymore...How lovely can spring get without the cherry blossoms? We'll follow your advice then!"

Genny was overly glad, "Awesome! I'll have all accommodation and programs extended accordingly. The children are going to love it! Thank you, Sister Celestine! I'll get the comprehensive information about their highly anticipated personalised Endearland's magical experience and journey delivered right up to you and all staff within the next ten minutes or so to your internet TV screen. This way everyone would be prepared and know what to expect. Also, satisfaction fully guaranteed!"

"Thank you so very much, Genny...For sure it will be the most memorable time for our children and us! We owe it all to you!" Sister Celestine expressed gratefully.

"No problem, thanks for leaving it all to us...We'll see you later!" Genny returned with a heart hopeful and brimming with excitement over a job well done.

3

A Nice Ride

"Oh, it's 'Believing the Future', our family's old-time favourite!" Genny smiled with pleasure to herself as the car radio began playing the mesmerising song. She was driving down the countryside highway from her home at a little below the maximum speed limit of 90km/hour, thoroughly enjoying the strong breeze of the early morning blowing hard against her hair and skin, made possible with the modified hybrid four-wheel-drive jeep's open roof.

She turned the volume more than thrice louder and hummed along with the singer's nearly-all-perfect vocals. The lyrics was enough to bring in touching and unforgettable memories, as though narrating a dramatic life story. In the midst of the deep fondness and brimming happiness, Genny reminded herself with determination not to shed any tear. After so many years, she knew very well that God has been good to her and everyone who is dear and precious in her life. He has rewarded her with many valuable experiences and successes, too wonderful to be stated in mere words. Nevertheless, it was not the end yet, for she still has much more dreams and vision that lie within the bottom of her heart, awaiting to be shared with loved ones and fulfilled with the help of the Heavenly Father above. She has faith to expect the best from Him...

The vehicle's built-in phone system sounded with an incoming call. Genny glanced at the caller's identity on display and was glad. She hit a button beside the radio volume one to answer it.

"Hey, you just wrapped up the conference meeting?" She beamed with delight.

Over at his office, he replied with a heartfelt smile, "Of course, can't wait to listen to you once again...How's my old pal performing? Does it meet your expectations?"

Genny chuckled at his seldom-expressed humour, "Oh, I'll give her a 120%! She's running extremely smoothly...Don't look down on her!"

Her description was enough to bring about a crease in his pair of thick eyebrows on an amused face.

He added innocently, "Come on, my car has never been given the role of an old girlfriend...Not like other guys...It's only a close buddy...Genny, don't overlook yourself, I mean it..."

She laughed even more, "Come on! I'm not jealous in any way, honest! Just that, cars have always been like that for guys...So I was just teasing you...Plus, she will always be your best sixteenth birthday present from Grandpa. I understand how much she means to you, even now...And, I do like her really!"

Jay broke into a soft laugh, "Okay, okay my princess...I just want to let you know the way I really regard my old buddy in my heart and I am glad that you understood me..."

Genny smiled at his straightforwardness, "Definitely, don't be hard on yourself...As for an update to not get you worrying unnecessarily again, I will soon be arriving at our Hush Coffee Library after another traffic light junction and a following left turn, taking only the next five minutes...Does that settle your heart?"

He nodded with less concern, "Sure, take care...If I can get this morning's pile of documents done by twelve noon, I just might be heading there to meet up with you..."

Genny knew that he could not help it, "No worries! I will still be waiting for you no matter which hour of the day so not to ever rush yourself...There's a whole day for me to relax before driving our E's townbus to pick up the children in the evening. I can't wait for them to enjoy the Fantasy Fireworks all around the Gardens estate tonight!"

He smiled at her pure excitement, "They're all ready and anticipating them...The children will love them for sure...Promise me to stay positive for it and not to worry..."

She was grateful that he gave his very best for them to have a lovely time and could not thank him enough. "Jay, thank you so much for everything," she expressed in bliss.

It warmed his heart, "As long as you are happy...I will be there..."

4

A Manageable Corner

Upon pushing the glass handle of the door open to enter her self-managed cafe library, Genny was refreshed by the sentimental charm of the piano instrumentals being played the moment she stepped inside. Her lips curved into a smile as the musical strings graced her ears. As usual, she was greeted by each employee who passed her by and they exchanged pleasant greetings with Genny. They were eager to congratulate her for the successful pre-screening of her latest animation collaboration. After a little talk here and there, Genny finally found time to proceed with her rounds of supervision.

She noticed familiar faces of young and old engaged in their reading at seats all about the place while enjoying intemitent sips of their favourite coffee beverage. There were also some who were gathered together in groups and they indulged in their delightful chatter banter of the day with one another. Genny was quick to spot that both the tall shelves and low side coffee tables were again half-emptied of books. It was time to connect with more publishers to ensure that the supply was not depleted. Keeping that in mind, she headed over to the beverage counter and saw that the chalkboard once more had her original honey latte item as the previous week best-seller. It seemed that without promotion of any sort, the classic drink was most-loved by nearly every cafe library member. Perhaps, as a thankful gesture, she should offer them for free during peak hours of the day. Or rather, she could accompany their orders with a unique souvenir gift. Given enough brainstorming, the liveliness of the place could be kept going.

She thought of taking out her mini notebook to start scribbling down those ideas. However, a light tap on her shoulder was felt the very next second, causing her to turn around in response. It was actually a recognisable face of a young teen member of the coffee library. Her expression spoke of that pure anticipation of a booklover she so often came across every day.

"Sis Genny, do you have that new release 'When Suddenly Becomes A Lifetime...' by Danson D.?" she asked with a tone of a whisper.

Genny immediately recalled that her once headstrong editor, now a professional as well as widely-celebrated author, did briefly inform the public of his latest work. She offered a warm smile and bent over to the girl's eye-level to answer her, "Anastasia, that new novel is coming, but there is still a month to go before its official debut...However, as for you our precious junior member, I can get the preview edition that has half of its full content delivered to your home or electronically by next weekend. You then can have the choice to purchase or return it later. How does that sound?"

Her face instantly lit up bright and full of cheer, "Thanks, Sis Genny, I can't wait! It's Valentine's next Saturday! That's Prince Charming Danson's most awesome gift for me!"

Genny was happy for her, "Wow, sounds like it's predestined...Well, enjoy the very best of February this year, sweetie! Shall I check in your books for today?"

She nodded contentedly and handed Genny her library books, "And I would love a cup of honey macchiato as well!"

Genny flashed an okay-sign, "I'll tell you what...Macchiatos are being offered doubled its regular portion at the same price for members who have their names beginning with the letter A today!"

"Great, yay!" She literally leapt for joy.

Following, everyone's ears perked up at Genny's words and came thronging towards the two like buzzing bees declaring their first and middle names to catch the deal. Both of them were all surrounded till the books almost fell off Genny's grip.

5

Ambition

"Goodness, more extensions? It's like we will never be getting 'enough' of our Endearland's dream! Jay, how shall I describe your unsurpassable ambition?" Genny remarked dreamily as she looked up from those gigantic sheets of design drafts and project proposals which Jay has excitedly set on the coffee table between them. He had earlier arrived with this awesome news at her coffee library and could not wait to discuss all the details with her.

He smiled at her with a charming gaze of anticipation over a cup of freshly-brewed macchiato before adding, "It's more of describing 'us'...Remember that you once dreamt of four seasons' castles? Well, I am so glad you told me because it's apparent that our current just-opened inn village exceeds capacity, both buildings are well over-booked, venues for events have long waiting lists - all these are telling us that it's so right for God to bless us the early completion of this project!"

Genny who has been listening attentively to him raised an eyebrow and calmly crossed her arms. "Hmmm, I see..." she cooly added and then returned to study the papers. "Are you planning a 'castle hotel'?"

He nodded with pleasure, "Sure, what do you think?"

She skimmed through quickly with eyes still intently affixed, "Which princess will it be featuring?"

Jay thought briefly in silence and took a sip of his hot coffee mix, "I'll let you decide..."

Genny immediately stared up at him, "What? So this is 'that' question you said you have been wanting to ask me since on your way here?"

He nodded again with that earnest smile, "I'll let my princess decide for us..."

There was a faint blush on her cheeks and she gradually smiled, "How can this prince be spoiling her like that!"

He chuckled softly, "Genny, I just get the sense that this princess whom you are going to choose would be telling the story of the one destined to melt the stone-cold heart of her rivals..."

"Oh," Genny grinned. "I kinda feel the same way...Did you eavesdrop on my thoughts?"

He smiled yet again and shrugged, "Perhaps, God just did a short-cut and whisper them straight to my ears?" Genny could not resist herself from punching him hard in the arm.

6

A Change

"Trinna, from the moment you stepped into the cafeteria, I had suspected it, and now I am so overjoyed for you – another perfumed bracelet from Chris!!" Genny could not stop staring at the scent-emanating jewel that her good friend now wore on her slender wrist. She smiled, as it reminded her of her very own unique musical ring from Jay.

Trinna beamed, "Genny, I never thought such a thing could possibly be created in real life...But, do you think he overdid it this time? I just can't imagine how many endless hours of tough work he put into making this thing a reality. I asked him how he did it, but he just responded that he had been thinking about me while working on this. How strange. I wonder if his brain must have been overworked..."

Genny giggled at her friend's tenderheartedness and squeezed Trinna's hands as she began talking excitedly, "Now, do you feel it? This is wishes overcoming stressful effort! Oh pure, sweet jasmine flower scent – I can't resist it either! It's no coincidence that Jay and Chris are cousins – they put in their all to emphasise such deep commitment. So Trinna, don't you ever take back your word in accepting Chris's concert arrangements again and don't extend the wait."

Trinna blushed and began discussing what she had planned for their afternoon date. "All right, all right, I surrender. It's not an easy thing to agree to, you know – after working so much for my school and career, I just feel uneasy about committing myself to a cause again." She sighed and continued, "I don't know, it just seems too fantasy-like!"

Genny smiled and shook her head. It seemed like her friend needed some encouragement. "Trinna, come on, you gotta be brave and get used to it! Chris is overly devoted to you and he's proven that!" She pointed to the bracelet to emphasise her point.

Trinna sighed again. "Genny, what's it like to be Jay's fiancée? And don't just lecture me; when are you both taking the next step?"

"Hmmm," Genny pondered for a second or two before shrugging. "I don't feel any different from who I used to be...In fact, I am not even aware of this role or identity a major part of the time! Isn't this strange?"

"Huh?" Trinna turned to her friend, a very confused expression on her face. "A question for a question...Genny, if this is how most engaged couples feel, then I am definitely not going to regret this!" She snapped her fingers and smiled widely, her expression full of confidence.

Genny grinned back and nodded excitedly, "Trinna, I am so glad for you. Now I'll get straight down to business and reserve your performance venue – Grand Ballroom, right?"

A waitress arrived, bringing their macchiato and rose tea. The girls expressed their thanks and helped themselves to the drinks.

Trinna nodded. "Genny, thanks for that. However, I really wanna do something special for this occasion."

"What's that?" asked Genny, leaning forward in curiosity.

"That is," Trinna grinned, "I want to turn the occasion into a costume event!"

Genny's eyes widened in surprise, but she couldn't stop the grin from forming on her own face. "What kind of a costume event?"

"Simply an engaging costume and ball event!" Trinna declared proudly.

7

To Dream

"Alice...or Ella or.....?" Trinna started flipping through her most handy companion, her personal designer's sketchbook as she pressed Genny for her answer.

After being done with her animated feature collaboration and the detailed arrangement of the orphanage children's stay at Endearland, Genny thought another big occasion to plan for would take a mentally heavy toll on her. What more with Jay's ambitious extension projects...Nevertheless, Genny was adept at concealing her weariness and wore a willing smile of gladness for her good friend's decision.

"Trinna, I am not saying me, but don't you think it's really a huge task to design each costume personally for every single guest to your concert event? Are you sure it won't stress you out since we are already public figures in the society?" She wanted to make sure Trinna was not undertaking an impossible mission for herself.

Inside her newly-renovated work studio situated a block or two away from her school, Trinna pressed a bow-shaped wall button and the music in the area switched to the song, 'My Destiny.'

She smiled understandingly, "Genny, remember that you and Jay once shared with us that one of the first themes in your proposal was to regularly hold a grand ball in Endearland for everyone who were in search of their dreams?"

Genny never expected that an idea gradually long forgotten and set aside would be recalled by Trinna so accurately this moment. She tried to recap, "Well, it sounds like so...but the funny thing is, I don't know exactly how such a plan came to be discarded...Could it be disagreement with the major investors then,...lack of preparation, organisation and.....?"

Trinna shook her head to dismiss Genny's concerns and held her hands to assure, "Don't be troubled by the bygones...Genny, will you allow me and Chris to resurrect this little well-guarded dream of yours?"

She looked hesitantly at her for a brief moment of silence. Trinna's face was filled with positive and brimming expectation. Genny then questioned, "Trinna, you're saying that you plan to turn your success event into a 'royals' ball event for all of us?"

She nodded excitedly, "Bingo! Even for those unknown princesses out there who would never dare to dream of one day that they will be attending a ball at your inn estate, I want them to know that favour is out there looking and searching for them! I want them to experience the reality of magic and fulfillment of their happiness..."

Genny broke into a soft chuckle of delight, "Trinna, how's that possible?"

She squeezed her hands gently, "That's why we need great planners like you and Jay to make these dreams come true...Genny, will you agree to this?"

Genny's eyes and smile turned dreamy as she considered before giving a little nod, "Uhmm...You sure can win my heart over..."

8

❦

Directions

The next morning, seated at her study table with french windows open wide before her that overlooked the breathtaking view of her home garden against the backdrop of scenic blue mountains, Genny nearly got carried away with her emotions while brainstorming for her proposal. It happened for at least a half-hour before she willed herself to snap out of her directionless mind-wandering and quickly got down to business...Scratching her temple with the rubber tip of her pencil, she frowned upon looking back down at the empty page of her notepad.

She leaned back against the comfort of her chair and sighed, "Shall I do more research on this, or simply start from scratch?"

She slid her pencil through the thick bun of her hair she tied up at the back of her head and folded her arms to recall just anything in the past she ever came across that was related to the a fairy-tale princess story...

After a brief minute of futile thinking, she changed her mind and shook her head. "Nah...I do believe that there are indeed many many modern-day princesses out there, but they just won't present themselves to you at the mere sound of a trumpet, unlike the narcissistic step-sisters...We should make use of a more implicit approach..."

She scribbled a few lines of such an idea down on the paper, her small lips curving into a grateful smile...

Following, she gave one of her cafe library assistants a call...

"Hello, Jocelynne? It's me...I just have a plan for an upcoming, and rather unprecedented promotion event for our library!" Genny added excitedly.

"Really? What's that, Sis Genny? I have opened up my processor program and ready to type it in any moment!"

Genny grinned, "I would like to organise a month-long free library membership program for anyone, plus giving away quantities of our book supply to the public, affiliated societies and charities. I am also open to suggestions, particularly from you, of practically any other way in which I can distribute our materials to as many people as possible..."

Jocelynne gasped in half disbelief, "Sis Genny, you serious? It's only 7:30 in the morning...Have you had breakfast? Or do you need me to buy you some jumbo sandwiches, or egg muffins or.....?"

Genny giggled softly, "Lynne, no worries...I am actually working on another lengthy proposal and to test out whether it will work for real...I need to implement this pilot promotion plan...but I can't reveal to you all its details yet because of a friendship promise. They can't go public at the moment but when the time is right, you just may be one of the first persons to know, okay?"

The girl was still concerned about her but despite her doubts, she thanked Genny for her clarification.

After they had hung up, Genny then contacted Aerine...

*****

"What? Me drawing sketches again? Genny, I told you many times that you are a much better drawer than me, and I....."

Genny quickly interrupted her, "Aerine, you did receive Trinna's request for her costume ball event proposal, right? Don't worry, it's only at least three rough sketches(can be in pencil) of your imagination of how our modern-day princesses would look like...And I am not imposing this task on you alone as I will be drawing as well...Later, I might also ask this from Trinna and Reanne, after she returned from Japan to-morrow..."

Aerine raised a curious eyebrow, "Huh? Miss Genny, what are you up to this time? This is part of your proposal draft?"

Genny beamed with confidence as she affirmed, "Yep, exactly! I will have all of your sketches printed out and distributed!"

Aerine was more confused, "I thought that we are not supposed to reveal this project to the public? Are you going to make Trinna mad, Genny?"

She sighed and waved a finger, "No, no, no...I will brainstorm and list down all the implicit qualities and attitudes of a modern-day princess, but definitely not mentioning that proposal along with the sketches, mind you..."

Aerine frowned a bit and remarked in a questioning tone, "That sounds like a lot of work, Genny...Are you sure you can handle all that?"

Genny considered, resting her chin on her palm as she replied, "I know, Trinna's too ambitious this time...But it's her first concert event. She not only wants herself to be happy, but that the world can be as happy as her.....Aerine, how about if we join forces and work as a group of two?"

Her face instantly lit up and she eagerly agreed, "Awesome idea, Genny! Can we suggest this to Trinna right away then?"

"Huh? As in now?" Genny turned hesitant but still hoped for the best that Trinna would consent.

9

Enriching Thoughts

"Let's see...My list of dispositional qualities for a fairy-tale princess would be someone who is patient; hopeful; loyal; filial; tender-hearted; soft-spoken...and...more to come soon...Then, the situational factors would be having too little time to do too many things; domineering people getting in the way of one's goals and dreams; too limited in resources to fulfill ambitions...and...more to come later..." Genny jotted down on her pocket notebook while she brainstormed during her casual walk down a street not far off from her cafe library. Taking morning strolls not only helped increase her energy level for the day, but also stimulated her mental creativity in order to come up with fresh new ideas and planning. Coming to a small park by the street, she took a glance at her wristwatch and smiled at the fact that it was still a quarter to ten, giving her a little extra time to savour before heading to her cafe.

She sat down on the concrete seat surrounding a tiny fountain in the middle of the park. Her hands still holding onto her notebook and an often-used pen, which was also a gift for her from Jay, she silently enjoyed the dewy scent of the morning and stared up at the bright blue open skies above, which was lit up strongly by the heartwarming midspring sunshine...Genny just loved such moments like this to slow down her pace in life and to reflect on the goodness of creation all around her...

Her dreamy impulse kicked in again and she found herself being inspired to write something out of the ordinary...She began to outline a story...

"...It was the night of Wendy's thirteenth birthday and she was patiently awaiting her parents and brothers' return from attending the school play performance. She was all alone at home and out of boredom, went into the kitchen and opened up the fridge to have another check at a lovely cake which she had prepared with her mother for herself earlier that day...It was an awesome creation by the two of them. Wendy could not resist carefully taking it out and placing it on the dining table, admiring the cake in an expectant manner..."Just a minute will do," she whispered calmly to herself as she sat infront of it with anticipation, before realising that she ought to ready some candles...She wondered if the cake would have space for all thirteen candles and hastily went to fetch them from the pantry drawer.

After getting them and breathing relief, she began considering where on the cake she would dip her first birthday candle...Peering intently, she squinted her eyes upon observing something peculiar..."When has this short candle's turned so out of shape?" She wondered in disturbing confusion and curiosity...To her astonishment, the dancing slender and pointy candle started leaping all about the moment she lifted her gaze to the lights on the ceiling above her, causing Wendy to gasp in utter startlement. The piece of candle she was holding in her hand at first dropped and appeared to stay mysteriously afloat by itself with a dust of twinkle before slowly settling down to push itself down onto the middle of the cake right above her pretty name.

When she was momentarily aware of what happened, she snapped herself out of a slightly dizzy spell and glanced back to behold her cake. Wendy immediately jerked and stepped backward in alarm, nearly knocking over the chair behind her and made her trip, but a hand caught hold of her in time to steady the baffled girl once again...All those weird tricky visions which occurred in a sudden gave her much lightheadedness and she has to rubbed her eyes hard to see with more clarity and certainty this time..."Oh, Cornelius! It is you, Cornelius? This isn't a dream, is it? You're here..." Once she has regained her footing, he stepped back slightly and bowed before her eyes. Wendy gaped and clasped her hands in delight...

"Happy Mother's day, my lady..." He greeted with a playful smile.

Wendy was still ever amazed by his presence, "Oh, ...today is not Mother's-..."

Before he could stress his words and clarify for her, something appeared to be forcefully pulling on his hat. "Why you...Can't you ever learn to stay still?" He spun around and tugged on tightly to his precious headgear.

Wendy gasped again, "Oh dear, it's your candle friend this time too, Cornelius?"

He grimaced and retorted, "No way is 'he' my friend, or rather, I dislike 'its' rebellious personality..."

Wendy stifled a giggle and switched her focus back to her cake, making sure it was still safe from their 'power struggle' so that she should put it back into the fridge as soon as possible...Yet, she was further surprised by the short pink candle now transforming through a sparkling golden flurry into double its original height and appeared as an odd-looking sharp-ended 'wand'...

Wendy was now dumbfounded and hurriedly called on Cornelius. His 'slender friend' has now freed its owner to wander again wildly in an unrestrained manner from one end of the wall to the other, irritating Cornelius as he crossed his arms and approached Wendy at the table.

She was earnestly pressing him for an explanation of her candle's disappearance and replacement when Cornelius grabbed her wrist in time before she carelessly pricked her finger on the sharp tip of the 'inverted magic wand'..."Careful," he whispered and hushed her with a knowing grin...Wendy obediently nodded and brought her finger against her lips as a gesture that she would listen to him. He then did a loud snap of his fingers with his free hand and hinted for them to wait...In about three seconds after, the wand automatically lifted itself up from the cake amidst blinding glittering dust and hovered in the air before revealing its bottom end to be that of a hole of a needle...It turned itself upright again and very slowly flew over to Wendy's side, surprising her greatly. She looked questioningly at Cornelius, who then said, "May I have the honour of you, my lady, to sew this defiant button back to my waistcoat again?"

Wendy wondered in awe at the piece of oversized needle-wand just about her arm's length that was now waiting for her to take possession of itself. "Oh my, I was not expecting this...Cornelius, I am not sure that I can use this, and I...I..."

Present...

A huge splashing sound of water from the fountain behind Genny's back diverted her indulgent mind back to the reality of the surroundings around her...She turned and immediately got up in shock. There, not far away from where she stood, was seen a little boy who has just thrown himself into the fountain and seemed to be bending over shakily searching for something deep inside the waters...Genny flung her book and pen aside and quickly loosened the straps of her sandals to rush over to his side...

10

A Suddenly

"Yes, newsroom? Our feature length animated movie topping the charts over its first week of theatrical release...So scheduling talks are now underway for the show to open in elsewhere within this month...Oh, great...just wonderful! Miss Genny would be thrilled to know this...Thanks so much, I'll let her know right away!" Jocelynne, as Genny's most capable round-the-clock assistant was extremely glad for her superior. The moment she hung up on this call by the doorway of her office at the rear of the cafe library, she hastily punched in Genny's cellphone number to get in touch right away.

Smiling from ear to ear, she awaited in great anticipation to break the news. However, her excitation soon died down as fast as they emerged about a minute ago...

"Isn't available right now? She turned off her phone at a time like this? How could this be?" Jocelynne ended the call, suspicious if she had keyed in the wrong number. She redialed again and the same automated message was repeated.

"Oh dear, she's usually on her way here at this hour..." Jocelynne murmured with deep furrowed brows. Throwing her phone back into her backpack, she flung the straps of her bag in a rough indignant manner over her shoulder and spun around in an attempt to rush down the hallway.

"Urgh...!" She rubbed her painful reddened forehead after knocking strongly onto a fellow barista staff the moment she rashly turned a sharp corner.

"Miss Jocelynne, I'm sorry, but now you look at what happened..." The cold unpleasantness in his voice sounded like announcing a disastrous aftermath.

She grimaced over the discomfort and opened her eyes again, only to be greeted by the sight of half-a-dozen large size marshmallow lattes dropped from a tray he was holding and the drinks now spilled all over a nearby trolley of new release books placed by the wall of the hallway.

Jocelynne's eyes widened in utter shock and devastation. "Wh-...What are these things doing here?!" She wailed and slumped on her knees before the piles of books intended for the library. Those long-awaited pre-orders now have brownish yellow liquid splattered on their covers and page edges, thoroughly horrifying Jocelynne.

She shakily reached out with one hand to finger the ill-fated materials, expression crestfallen and mouthing below a whisper with dread of the books' title, "When Suddenly Becomes A Lifetime,.....by Danson...D...Oh Lord, my 'suddenly' for today has turned into an inescapable bad break!"

II

An Inexpensive Wish

After an extremely wet incident at the park, Genny took the little boy who was accompanied by no one else with her. Together, they went to have a change at a nearby elite departmental store. She bought for him and herself new clothes. Her thoughtful gesture delighted him greatly and now he was dressed in a smart sky blue blazer underneath striped red and grey cotton shirt with dark indigo pants in place of of just a pale creased singlet and khaki shorts about an hour ago. His once pair of faded rubber flip-flops was now turned into cleanly polished brown leather shoes. Beaming with glee up at her, he gratefully offered his thanks.

All smiles and clasping his little hands, the boy expressed, "Thank you, my 'Fairy Big Sister'...You made my wish come true. But I don't know why you look different from my cartoon show...You wear a yellow t-shirt and blue jeans? Yesterday, I wished for nice new clothes and shoes for a new year and now, they appeared! I am so happy because of picking up my small coin from the fountain pool! What mother's said is true!"

Genny tried her best to keep her smile, amidst realising this little boy sounded really clever and observant for his age. She bent over to meet his eye level and asked patiently, "Smartie boy, I am only a modern Godsister, see that I have no wings on my back...But now, I would like to ask you, why did mommy say that you have to get back your wishing coin from the fountain?"

He pursed his lips a little to ponder before revealing, "Ah! Mommy said that God would give poor people a discount for making our wishes at the fountain. He would only charge us a nickel for one night and we can take it back in the morning...Isn't this wonderful?"

Genny felt so touched listening to his innocent sweet voice. She softly patted his head and blinked back tears, "Surely God has answered your wish, right? Do you like your new clothes and shoes? Why don't we head over to that restaurant at that corner for a breakfast feast? And can you tell this godsister what your name is?"

He grinned wide and answered, "Thank you so much, Fairy Godsister...My name is Peter Park..."

"Peter Park?" Genny was amused by his sweet innocence.

He gave a strong nod, "Mhmm! My father and mother have just gotten their new jobs as a gardener and maid in a giant palace last Christmas...That is why they cannot be at home all day today."

"Huh? Giant palace?" Genny was once again confused by his description. She thought for a second and was about to inquire more from him when their attention was interrupted by some lady's loud scolding voice near the entrance door of the departmental store.

"Can't you stop being so absent-minded?! You're young but I am old! Just look at you, always forgetting to bring our shopping lists! Don't expect me to carry all these bags for you, it's your mistake and you got to pay for it! I'll move on to the basement supermarket!" She literally lashed out like a terrible merciless judge at a girl who was struggling to grasp onto more than a dozen of bags packed and filled to the brim with items that they were nearly falling out. The unfeeling lady then turned her back on the girl and paced swiftly past the store as well as Genny and the child, treating them like invisible air before stepping onto the escalator close by that would take her to the lower level of the mall.

In an effort to catch up with her stern boss lady, the girl, who was somewhere in her mid-twenties, unknowingly slipped on the string handles of one of the heavy bags on the mosaic floor and stumbled clumsily in a disheveled heap with a load of tangled items.

Upon noticing what had happened to her, Genny and the little boy were overly concerned and quickly rushed over to help her up.

12

Urgency

Since the terrible mistake she had committed a while ago, Jocelynne decided that she would not dare to face Genny until she has gotten everything settled, so she turned off her cellphone.

She brought all those badly wet and stained books with her out of the cafe and went to sit and wait outside a book-cleaning store for over an hour. It was still closed and seemed to delaying opening at its usual stated hours, causing Jocelynne's fear that it would be closed for the day. Staring worriedly and crestfallen at the pile of spoilt books stacked inside a whole box placed on the ground before her, she has to willfully inhibit herself from shedding a self-pity tear or two.

"Please...please...I can't lose this job," she begged in whispering tone while looking up at the heavens, about to break down any moment. Since being hired by Genny a few years ago and now, as her personal assistant for the cafe library as well, she had fulfilled all her assignments smoothly without any large-scale irrecoverable error of this sort. This second, she still could not contain fully her devastated conscience. She was about to shut her eyes and succumbed to utter doom and gloom when a wave of hand right before her startled Jocelynne out of her depressing cycle of emotions and thoughts.

"Young lady, have you been waiting for my store?" An elderly man asked her.

"Oh uh..." Jocelynne immediately got up from a short wooden stool placed by the shop's front door, which was most probably supplied by the caring old man. She pleaded with a stammer, "Please, Sir...I desperately needed to get these books here cleaned to their original state...I'm nearly out of hope, only you can help me...Please..."

He looked at her thoughtfully for a few brief seconds before giving a light nod and went over to her box load of materials. Bending over, he picked up one of the books and examined its inside. In a moment, he remarked plainly, "The fibres are all coming off that it's going to be very tough...The pages would be thinned to an extreme degree...But, I see that you have the heart for these books, wanting to preserve them despite the easier choice of disposing everything...All books are precious and an original masterpiece...Kind lady, I will do my best...However, if urgency is an issue, then..."

Jocelynne's face instantly lit up like the glare of the morning sun. She quickly added, "Thank you so very much, Sir...May I know how can I compensate you for your saving work?"

The store owner apologetically revealed that he would make the exception to take on her request only if she could convince his priority customer to delay his deadline of completing his same-day work on behalf.

"It would be better if you could even personally talk to him over the phone because it has always been hard for me to converse with him without getting into disagreements," he requested candidly.

Jocelynne gratefully volunteered without a second thought and the owner of the store rang up his number.

"Hello, Mr Song? Morning, how have you been doing?..." After a very concise greeting and opening, he handed the phone over to Jocelynne.

"Err...Hi, Mr So-ng...? I am extremely sorry to bother you at this time, but I understand that you are a frequent customer of...Perfect-Flash Book Cleaning Services...My name is Jocelynne and I totally regret to say that I have an urgent need to get a hundred copies of books done by today. Please do not blame Perfect-Flash store owner because I am the one who pleaded with him to handle my books before yours...I apologise that this would cause you unnecessary delay but I promise that I would make up for it...So can you please..."

"What's with all these nonsense?!" He literally lashed out at her. "I placed my request 24 hours ago and do you know how time is much more precious to me than money?!"

Jocelynne was simply chilled to the bone by his response. Turning panicky, she was at a lost for words.

"No excuse to offer? I won't buy any of them anyway," he did not give her a chance to sound a word before hanging up on her.

Jocelynne's face paled and now definitely, tears started welling up in her eyes until she has to sob hard to prevent them, yet to no avail.

The old man shook his head and came over to softly pat her shoulder compassionately.

He graciously suggested, "Young lady, that's just him - unyielding and would never fall back on his stone-cold principles...But, perhaps, you could help me with handling part of his job so we can kill two birds with one stone...? I'll pay you for your work..."

Jocelynne lifted her watery gaze once again and hastily rubbed her eyes dry. "Really, Sir? Oh, I am not expecting this in the least...This is more than I could ever hope for...Not to worry, I won't need a single penny from you...Can we get started?"

He laughed heartily and gestured for them to bring all her books into the store as he got out his heavy bundle of keys to open the door. However, the 'closed' sign remained unturned since they would not be able to take on further cleaning request for the whole day.

13

Unexpected

It was early afternoon and Trinna has been impatiently awaiting Chris's arrival for their tea date of the week in a cottage restaurant. She was rather let down by him being unusually behind schedule and extremely unlike his timely attitude. She began to get slightly worried and was about to give him another call when the tall gentleman showed up at last pushing through the crowded door amidst a group of upper-class elderly ladies.

Checking the time, she worked out that he was forty minutes and thirty seconds late, more than his first record of half an hour, which happened shortly after they first got together and started dating.

Upon reaching their table, he offered an awkward smile after all that hectic rush. Trinna was unsure of whether to return him with the same expression and so merely nodded at him just once. Deep inside, the insecurities aroused within her and she wondered with concern whether he was being slack already after she has just agreed to their first concert event.

"Have you thought about our latest project proposal?" She dived straight to the point.

Chris hastily sat down and added absent-mindedly, "How's this week's rose tea special? Did you like it?"

Trinna's sweatdropped and mentally switched to a judgemental mode to contemplate about him not treating their latest proposal seriously. Added to that, she has not even ordered a single cup of rose tea but chose to try out jasmine tea for the day. Meanwhile, he was about to consider explaining to her why he was not on time for the day but only ended up sighing while inadvertently glancing at a folder sticking out of his half-zipped bag. The earlier intention forgotten, he opted to stuff the thick set of documents further inside it.

Observing his unheeding reaction to her current top priority, Trinna decided that she could not spare more time for tea with him and preferred to leave for her school in disappointment. Grabbing her handbag, she turned about without a second look and neither a parting word for the unexpected Chris. Instead, she paced swiftly out of the restaurant.

He was taken aback by her leaving and let out a baffled sigh. For some reason, he was quite unlike his usual jovial self and was rather slow to reach a quick decision to go after her...

*****

At his office, Jay set aside the documents which were related to a meeting held earlier with representatives of his company to discuss further plans of their Endearland Gardens extensions and construction of castle-like building. It did not go on as smoothly as the way he had intended and imagined previously with positive hope, which now brought down his confidence.

Leaning back against his leather chair, he paused for a moment of thought. He knew of criticisms and backtalk by others that he was not a person who welcomed advice without reservation and tended to cut them off very easily. Yet, staunch and defiant as he has always been, Genny still accepted this weakness of his almost unconditionally. She may not always take sides when he protested of such problems with her, but she could be gracious enough to offer him warm comfort and strength to do his very best.

His gaze trailed over to the centre of the far side of his work table, where he has placed a silver plated-framed photo of Genny and him when they both dressed up in a cosplay costume outside their recently-completed inn estate. His lips curved into a contented smile. He figured that he would like to head over to Genny's cafe library to unwind and be her barista for the day.

I4

Coincidence

"Daisy! You are and must be Daisy!" Genny exclaimed excitedly upon coming up face to face to help the fallen pitiful young lady.

The little boy was clever enough to untangle the whole bunch of string handles of those shopping bags in less than a minute, enabling the girl to easily get up on her feet with Genny's light assistance.

She heaved a deep sigh of exhaustion and patted her skirt, "Why, thank you so very much...Miss Genny Lee and you dearest sweetie..."

She was about to take up all those heavy bags again when Genny insisted that she would offer a hand to carry some of them and this gesture of honour greatly touched the girl.

"I know you still recognise me, so please call me exactly the way you did before when we first met during our freshman year!" Genny emphasised as she led them to walk past the store.

She smiled modestly, "Oh, thank you, Genny...I miss calling you that...You haven't changed the slightest!"

She nodded, "So glad to hear that from you, Daisy...But before I forget, what's with that stern lady a while back? She treated you in an extremely mean way!"

The girl cast a downward gaze before replying, "She's my old company's creditor and now my boss...Don't blame her, it's always been like this..."

Genny quickly stopped in her track and turned Daisy's shoulder to face her. "Hey, Daisy! You were known as the 'DAring Intelligent Smart Youth' back in school...Why are you acting so different now?!"

She lifted a hesitant gaze, "After you left our school to lead the elite life, I flunked almost all my courses and dropped out of university. I've not been able to land a job ever since and so rely a great deal on my parents' savings to start a very small company. As you may have guessed, things didn't work out with mountains of debt. Of course, we have to do our best to ensure that we do everything for our creditor..."

Genny's heart was gradually filled with empathy for her and she thought silently to herself, "An overbearing stepmother-like creditor bossy lady...Hmmm...God must be showing something to me here..."

While Genny was absent-mindedly indulging in her contemplation, Daisy simply shrugged off her miserable life issues and raised a doubting eyebrow to inquire softly, "Err...sorry if this should offend you...but...is he your unknown 'nephew'?"

Genny's eyes rolled big and then broke into an uncontrollable fit of laughter. She then waved her hands agitatingly and proudly introduced to Daisy, "He is Peter Park, my new friend!"

Daisy was surprised, "Peter...or Peter Park? Oh anyway, you're a very good-looking young master...Here's a little peppermint candy for ya!"

"Thank you, Fairy Godsister's friend!" He expressed with irresistible sweetness.

Following, she came to her realisation and informed Genny that she has to get back to her bossy boss before she lost her temper while searching for her. They bade goodbye and parted ways right after Daisy left Genny her contact number. Seeing her rushing like crazy, Genny shook her head as she held on to Peter's hand. She figured that her first 'princess' has appeared...

15

Task Completion

After a half-day of tough work, Jocelynne could finally finished cleaning her assigned portion of ten 1000-page books. She took off her apron and sat down by the front counter of the store. Heaving a deep sigh of relief, she put on a grateful smile and whispered a word of thanks to her God above. Her gaze rested on the fruits of her labour piled up neat and orderly inside a box placed on the counter before her. The covers were all in a condition better than new as she now got the chance to observe while picking one up and very slowly turned the pages with her handgloves on. She experienced an overwhelming sense of accomplishment and her smile turned brighter with each passing second. Unable to contain her utter gladness, she shut her eyes and hugged the book snugly against her chest, basking in the positive hope that her load of newly-released books for Genny's cafe would be ready to be brought back in just a little short amount of time, as promised by the store owner.

Opening her gleaming pair of eyes, they were greeted by another pair of irresistible ones gazing unwaveringly back at her, startling Jocelynne out of her wits as she immediately jerked backwards and threw the thick book out of her arms, coincidentally hitting straight at that person in the process. She instinctively backed up but forgetting that she was actually seated on a high chair behind the counter, she almost clumsily fell over but his strong steady hand managed to grab her wrist momentarily to buy time for her to regain footing.

"Oh...my...bad...You scare the heavens out of me!" Jocelynne felt a little dizzy due to the sudden appearance of the stranger customer. She sighed and checked all over to make sure that the books were not in any way affected by the unexpected incident. It was then that the young man presented the copy which struck him seconds ago towards her anxious face.

Jocelynne stared up at him, who playfully smirked at her goofiness. "Why, thank you...This is really priceless, you know...I must ensure that not a single one of them is missing..." She added candidly.

He lightly nodded and leaned one side forward against the counter, watching her thoughtfully as she swept off with her fair palms every speck of dirt and dust from the hardcover gently, then blowing at the outer edges of the pages before giving further the whole book a few more soft pats and carefully sliding it downwards into a little free space at one corner of the box to fit in with the rest of its companions.

"Ah there...all done," she smiled with satisfaction and lifted her gaze.

A subtle blush colored her cheeks. He let out another faint smile at her this time, causing Jocelynne to be annoyed at a lost for words.

"Oh, you're here...but still an hour early!" An elderly voice calling from the rear of the store interrupted their brief exchange.

The man whom Jocelynne quietly guessed to be in his late twenties now turned from her to face the approaching store owner and responded bluntly, "I thought of discussing with you my change of 'unreasonable' decision to get my books back later the next day...But it seems to be not at all necessary as of now..."

Jocelynne was stunned as she just perked her ears to listen to his every word. Gasping inaudibly, she was so not wanting to meet this cold and stiff-necked 'Mr So-ng'...

The owner now joined them at the counter, "Yes indeed as you've said...but the credit all goes to this young lady here...She is a fast and capable learner, working hard through all your books so I won't get an earful from you!"

Jocelynne was not anticipating these to come from that good old man in the least. She cast an uneasy glance at the young snobbish guy and shook her head nervously.

He simply shrugged but still looked impressed, "I suppose just that overused two words won't be enough for you both, right?"

The owner laughed deafeningly, "How can I ask for anything more from you?"

He spared a brief instant of silence before concluding, "Anything this young lady here may ask of me..." He purposefully turned his gaze towards her again to emphasise his firm tone.

Jocelynne could not help but stared back at him with eyes widened in surprise.

To be continued...

www.ingramcontent.com/pod-product-compliance
Lightning Source LLC
Chambersburg PA
CBHW070943120726
47908CB00005BA/1508